CONTENTS

The Library of Doom is a hidden fortress.
It holds the world's largest collection
of strange and dangerous books.

Behold the Librarian. He defends the Library – and
the world – from super-villains, clever thieves
and fierce monsters. Many of his adventures
have remained secret. Now they can be told.

SECRET #44
A BOOK IN THE WRONG HANDS
IS THE WRONG BOOK.

Chapter One

ON THE WALL

Near the Library of Doom stands a **HUGE** warrior of stone.

The stone figure is really another fortress. It is called Heroes Hold.

The statue's feet stand on a rocky island. The island is surrounded by a STORMY ocean.

Four mighty walls **CIRCLE** the Hold, one inside the other.

A young man keeps guard. He stands on the wall closest to the fortress.

It is the Iron Page. He wears armour the colour of **INK**.

Something moves in the shadows.

"Who's there?" asks the Iron Page.

"It's me," says a voice. A young woman floats out of the **DARKNESS**.

The woman has long, dark hair and wears a red suit. She is the Specialist.

The Specialist and the Iron Page help protect the LIBRARY OF DOOM.

"Bad news," says the Specialist. "Our old foe the **BEAST** has broken into the Hold."

"Impossible!" says Iron. "I haven't seen it anywhere."

The Specialist looks **WORRIED**.

"It's true. The Librarian sent me a **WARNING**," she says. "We must find a new hiding place for the Hold's treasure, before the Beast gets it."

Chapter Two

HALL OF HEROES

"We must **HURRY**," says the Specialist.

The Iron Page nods. He leads his friend into the fortress.

He pulls a small book from his armour. The book is called **SHORT STORIES**.

Iron throws it onto the floor.

The book grows longer and **WIDER**.
The cover opens to reveal a dark tunnel.

The Specialist jumps into the tunnel. The Iron Page jumps next.

The **SPECIAL** book shortens the distance they travel.

Luckily, the book also has a Plot Twist. The Twist turns the tunnel and points it upwards.

THOOOOMP!

The two have reached the highest storey in the Heroes Hold.

They are inside the stone statue's giant head. The room is made of pure GOLD.

It is the Hall of Heroes.

The golden walls are **COVERED** with life-sized figures.

Some figures hold swords and shields.
Others **FLY** through the air.

A growl suddenly ECHOES through the room.

GGHRRRRRRGGGGGG!

"What's that?" asks the Iron Page.

"The Beast," says the Specialist. "It's coming."

Chapter Three

FIRE AND WATER

The Specialist points to a golden corridor. At the end is a door made of black **FIRE**.

The flames *ROAR*.

"Beyond that fire lies the **TREASURE** the Beast wants," says the woman.

Could the creature get through the flames? wonders the Iron Page.

"We must get the **TREASURE** so we can hide it," says the Specialist. "But only the Librarian can pass through that fire."

"You forget. I can too," says Iron.

"That's right!" says the Specialist. "We can **USE** your shield."

Iron always carries a large shield of POLISHED metal on his back. He holds it out in front of him.

"Get behind me," he tells the Specialist.

The two heroes crouch down. They take a running leap towards the flames.

HIIIIIIIISSSSSSSSSSSSSSSSSSS!

The friends feel a **BURST** of heat. The shield protects them both from the flames.

They are inside a new room. A **GIANT** bubble of water lies ahead of them.

"Inside the water is the **TREASURE**. It's the book *Heroes*," says the Specialist. "It holds the powers of all heroes from every story."

If the Beast gets it, thinks Iron, *the villain will become more powerful than we can imagine.*

Chapter Four

IN THE BUBBLE

The Iron Page starts to move towards the **BUBBLE** of water. But the Specialist stops him from walking closer.

"I'll handle this," she says and steps into the bubble.

The bubble's wall is thick. The water whirls with the power of a WATERFALL.

It drags and pushes the Specialist to the top of the bubble.

The Specialist **THRUSTS** out her boots. They rip a hole in the watery wall.

She drops through the hole and enters the inner bubble of air. She lands on the ground.

A book lies on a table of ICE.

A **SINGLE** word fills its cover.

The young woman grabs the book.

The Specialist fights her way out of the **BUBBLE**. She holds the book tight.

"Hurry!" says the Iron Page. "We must leave before the **BEAST** comes."

The Specialist smiles and says, "It's already here."

Her face begins to **MELT**. She grows larger and larger.

"You are the **BEAST!**" shouts the Iron Page.

Chapter Five

BORROWING

The Beast laughs.

HA-HA-HA-HAAGGGGGHHHH!

"I borrowed the Specialist's face," it says. "Just as I will borrow all the POWERS of this book!"

The Beast knocks the Iron Page to the floor with its **MIGHTY** arm.

"Nothing will stop me now!" it shouts.

"I WILL!" says a voice.

The book of heroes FLIES out of the Beast's hand.

FFWWOOOOOOMMM!

The book lands on the floor. Feet shoot out from the book. Then a head.

The book **TRANSFORMS** into the Librarian.

"I was borrowing too," says the hero.

The Beast lunges at the Librarian with its POWERFUL claws.

The Librarian struggles in the Beast's tight grip. He frees one hand and **WAVES** his fingers.

A blast of **WIND** hurls the Beast backwards into the watery bubble.

Another wave of the hero's hand
turns the bubble to solid ICE.

The Beast is **TRAPPED**.

The Librarian **RUSHES** to the Iron Page.

The young man is still GROGGY from being hit.

"Librarian?" asks the Iron Page. "But where is the Specialist?"

"She's been **GUARDING** the walls this whole time," says the hero. "She's safe."

Iron can't wait to see the Specialist.

He'll tell her about the Librarian's amazing trick: He rose from *HEROES*.

GLOSSARY

borrow use something that belongs to someone else, with the idea that it will be returned later

foe enemy

groggy weak and not able to think or act normally, especially after sleeping or being knocked out

hold place made to be strongly protected against attacks

hurl throw with a strong force

lunge move or jump forward suddenly

page young worker

specialist someone who has special skills or knows a lot about something

storey floor of a building

transform change completely

TALK ABOUT IT

1. The Iron Page helps protect the Heroes Hold. Describe his character. How does he behave? What tools does he use?

2. Were you surprised when the Beast appeared? Why or why not? Look through the story for hints that the Specialist was not herself.

WRITE ABOUT IT

1. What other treasures might be hidden inside the Heroes Hold? Create your own treasure. Describe it and its powers.

2. There are many types of heroes, but they all work to help others. Who is your hero? Write two paragraphs about them. Make sure you explain why they are special to you.

ABOUT THE AUTHOR

Michael Dahl is an award-winning author of more than 200 books for young people. He especially likes to write scary or weird fiction. His latest series are the sci-fi adventure Escape from Planet Alcatraz and School Bus of Horrors. As a child, Michael spent lots of time in libraries. "The creepier, the better," he says. These days, besides writing, he likes travelling and hunting for the one, true door that leads to the Library of Doom.

ABOUT THE ILLUSTRATOR

Patricio Clarey was born in 1978 in Argentina. He graduated in fine arts from the Martín A. Malharro School of Visual Arts, specializing in illustration and graphic design. Patricio currently lives in Barcelona, Spain, where he works as a freelance graphic designer and illustrator. He has created several comics and graphic novels, and his work has been featured in books and other publications.